Wheels on the Bus

Illustrated by Gabriele Antonini

Published by Sequoia Children's Publishing,
a division of Phoenix International Publications, Inc.

8501 West Higgins Road
Chicago, Illinois 60631

59 Gloucester Place
London W1U 8JJ

© 2020 Sequoia Publishing & Media, LLC

Customer Service: cs@sequoiakidsbooks.com

www.sequoiakidsbooks.com

ISBN 978-1-6426-9041-5

The wheels on the bus go round and round,
Round and round, round and round.

The wheels on the bus go round and round,
All through the town.

The wipers on the bus go swish, swish, swish;
Swish, swish, swish; swish, swish, swish.

The wipers on the bus go swish, swish, swish,
All through the town.

The doors on the bus go open and shut,
Open and shut, open and shut.

The doors on the bus go open and shut,
All through the town.

The horn on the bus goes beep, beep, beep;
Beep, beep, beep; beep, beep, beep.

The horn on the bus goes beep, beep, beep,
All through the town.

The riders on the bus go up and down,
Up and down, up and down.

The riders on the bus go up and down,
All through the town.

The baby on the bus cries, "Wah, wah, wah;
Wah, wah, wah; wah, wah, wah."

The baby on the bus cries, "Wah, wah, wah,"
All through the town.

The mommy on the bus says, "Shush, shush, shush;
Shush, shush, shush; shush, shush, shush."

The mommy on the bus says, "Shush, shush, shush,"
All through the town.

The riders on the bus say, "Thanks for the ride;
Thanks for the ride; thanks for the ride."

The riders on the bus say, "Thanks for the ride;
All through the town."